VioLet

Written by Tania Duprey Stehlik

Illustrated by Vanja Vuleta Jovanovic

Second Story Press

Violet poked her nose out from under the blankets. This was the day she had been dreading ever since they'd moved into the new house.

"Rise and Shine!" her mom called from the doorway. "You don't want to be late on the first day of school."

"I don't feel so good," Violet moaned. "My stomach hurts."

"It's just a few butterflies," her mom said. "They'll disappear."

"Oh, it's worse than that. It's serious...maybe even contagious!"

"Nice try, Missy! But you're going. Up you get!"

So, Violet got up and ate her breakfast. Her lunch was made and sitting on the counter.

"I hope this is extra good so I can trade it with someone else," she said, packing the food inside her school bag. "It might help me make new friends."

"Oh, Violet," chided her mom, "just be yourself. You don't need to give away your lunch to make friends."

It couldn't hurt, Violet thought, as she dragged herself out the door behind her mom.

All the way to school, Violet's heart was pounding. She could see all the kids making their way to the front doors. There were red kids, yellow kids, and blue kids...and then there was Violet.

Her mom gave her a big hug. "Bye, sweetie. I know you'll have a great day, and don't forget, Dad will pick you up after school."

Violet walked slowly into the schoolyard, trying her best to fit in.

The day was a flurry of introductions, arts and crafts, and all sorts of interesting activities. Everyone seemed friendly, and Violet soon forgot about her butterflies. She even traded some of her lunch with a girl who asked to sit beside her in the cafeteria. Then, just like that, the school day was over.

Violet was out in the schoolyard looking for her dad. She hung out with her new classmates while she waited. They were red kids, yellow kids, and blue kids. She was telling them how nervous she had been that morning when her dad's car pulled up. He waved and motioned her over. "Come on," her dad called. "Let's go!"

"Who's that?!?" asked a girl from her class.
"That's my dad," replied Violet proudly.
"Your dad?!" The girl looked puzzled. "Your dad is BLUE??!"
"I guess so," answered Violet, wondering what she meant.
"Well...how come your dad is blue and you're not?"
Violet didn't know. The truth was, she had never thought about it before.
She shrugged and ran toward the car.

Violet was quiet all the way home. She was thinking about what the girl had said and worrying all over again about fitting in. Why wasn't she blue? Or red?

Mom was red. Dad was blue.
So, why wasn't she red or blue?
Come to think of it, all her red
friends had red parents. Her
yellow friends had yellow parents.
Her blue friends had blue parents.
So, why was she purple?

Violet's mom was waiting in the kitchen. "So, how was your day? Did you make any friends?" The tears started to stream from Violet's eyes. "What's wrong?" asked her mom, drying her face.

"Why am I not blue?" asked Violet.

"Ohhh," said her mom. "Did someone at school ask you that?"

Violet nodded.

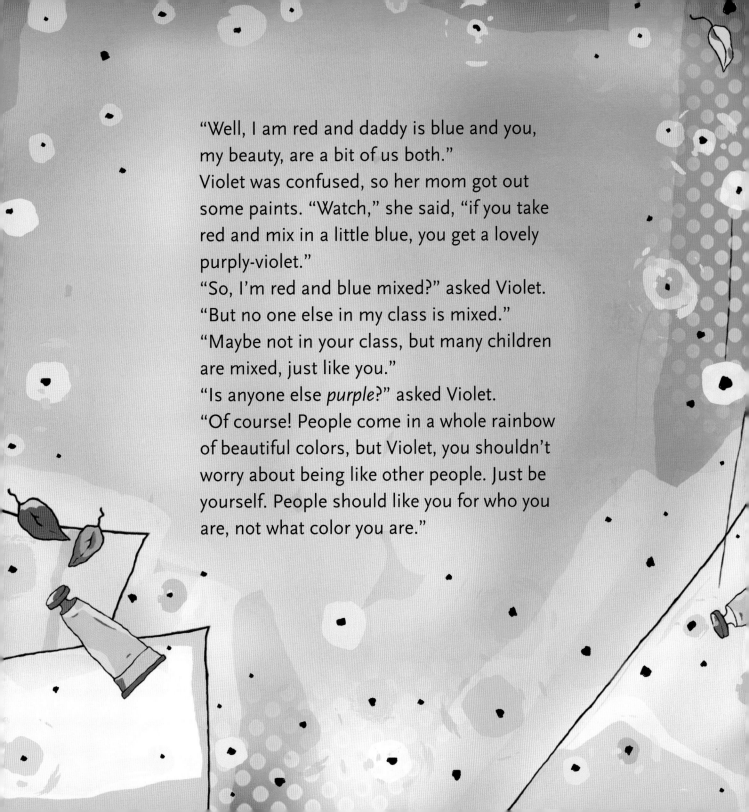

"Well, I am red and daddy is blue and you, my beauty, are a bit of us both."
Violet was confused, so her mom got out some paints. "Watch," she said, "if you take red and mix in a little blue, you get a lovely purply-violet."
"So, I'm red and blue mixed?" asked Violet. "But no one else in my class is mixed."
"Maybe not in your class, but many children are mixed, just like you."
"Is anyone else *purple*?" asked Violet.
"Of course! People come in a whole rainbow of beautiful colors, but Violet, you shouldn't worry about being like other people. Just be yourself. People should like you for who you are, not what color you are."

The next day went by just as fast as the first, and when school was over, Violet waited for her mom to pick her up.
"Who's that?" a boy from her class asked.

"That's my mom," said Violet as proud as ever. "Your mom is red?!" he asked, a little confused. "Yep!" she said. "My mom is red, my dad is blue, and *I*," she said, grinning...

"...am Violet!"

Library and Archives Canada Cataloguing in Publication

Stehlik, Tania, 1981-
Violet / by Tania Stehlik ; illustrated by Vanja Vuleta Jovanovic.

ISBN 978-1-897187-60-9

1. Racially mixed children--Juvenile fiction. I. Jovanovic, Vanja
Vuleta, 1979- II. Title.

PS8637.T435V56 2009   C813'.6   C2009-902559-0

Second Story Press gratefully acknowledges the support of the
Ontario Arts Council and the Canada Council for the Arts for our
publishing program. We acknowledge the financial support of
the Government of Canada through the Book Publishing Industry
Development Program.

Printed and bound in China

ONTARIO ARTS COUNCIL
CONSEIL DES ARTS DE L'ONTARIO

Canada Council   Conseil des Arts
for the Arts   du Canada

Published by
SECOND STORY PRESS
20 Maud Street, Suite 401
Toronto, Ontario, Canada
M5V 2M5
www.secondstorypress.ca

For my parents, Larry
& Mina, who have
lovingly guided me
thus far
— T.D.S.

To my family with
infinite love
— V.V.J.